Twintuity

A BOOK OF LOVE POEMS

Twintuity
A Book of Love Poems
All Rights Reserved
No part of this publication may be
reproduced, distributed, or transmitted
in any form or by any means, including
photocopying, recording, or other electronic,
or machanical methods, without the written
permission of the publisher, except as permitted
by U.S copyright law.
By
Melissa Alexander
©2024

To My Beloved

I THOUGHT OF YOU TODAY
IT BROUGHT ME A SMILE
NO MORE REGRETS
JUST WALKING OF MILES

YOUR EYES SING A SONG
IN THE EARS OF MY SOUL
YOUR LIPS ARE LIKE CANDY
A CHILD STEALS FROM A BOWL

YOUR SMILE LIGHTS MY PATH
IN THE DARK OF MY MIND
ALL MY FEAR AND MY ANGER
I AM LEAVING BEHIND

THANKFUL AND BRIGHT
AS I WALK IN YOUR LIGHT
MY ANGEL ON EARTH
YOU'RE MY TRUEST DELIGHT

I THOUGHT I SAW YOU
IN THE CROWD

MY MIND'S PLAYING
TRICKS ON ME

YOU'RE A THOUSAND
MILES AWAY

BUT IN

MY MIND
YOU'RE HERE
WITH ME

THEY SWITCHED US LIKE
AN APRIL FOOL

NOW YOU ARE ME
AND I AM YOU

MY PRETTY QUEEN
IS NOW A MAN

WHO HAS THE WORLD
INSIDE HIS HAND

AND I THE KING
NOW DRESSED IN PINK

A GENIUS MIND
FORCED NOT TO THINK

WHAT DID WE DO
THAT WAS SO WRONG?

IT'S A KARMIC CYCLE
JUST PLAY ALONG

OUR LOVE IS IN AUTUMN
THE BEAUTIFUL LEAVES

ARE SILENTLY FALLING
WITH EACH PASSING BREEZE

NO MORE BRIGHT SUN
OR CLEAR SUMMER DAYS

JUST RAINDROPS AND WIND
TO COME CLEAR LOVE AWAY

OUR BEAUTIFUL LOVE
GETTING READY FOR SNOW

WE'VE BEEN HERE BEFORE
OUR SHOVELS IN TOW

HOW PRETTY WE ARE
WE TRY TO HOLD ON

LIKE LEAVES ON A TREE
SOON OUR LOVE'
WILL BE GONE

MY HEAD
ON YOUR HEART
IT'S A
HEAVENLY BEAT

IT'S MY FAVORITE SONG
TO PLAY ON REPEAT

I LAY MY SOFT CHEEK
ON YOUR WARM
SILKY CHEST

YOUR HEART BEATS
FOR ME
SO THAT
MAKES IT THE BEST

I CANNOT TAKE
WHAT ISN'T MINE
LOOK DON'T TOUCH
'CAUSE LOVE IS BLIND

MOVE ON THEY SAY
AND DON'T LOOK BACK
JUST LOVE YOURSELF
YOU'LL NEVER LACK

BUT YOU ARE MINE
AND I AM YOURS
SINCE ANCIENT TIMES
THROUGH ANCIENT WARS

THE LOVE YOU SEEK
YOU'LL FIND IN ME
AS BIG AS HEAVEN
DEEP AS THE SEA

WE MADE A CHOICE
IT HAD TO BE
I LEARN FROM YOU
YOU LEARN FROM ME

PLASTIC DOLLS AND
GAMES WE PLAY
IT'S TIME TO THROW
THEM ALL AWAY

ATLEAST FOR ME
THAT'S HOW I FEEL
SO WHILE I WAIT
I'LL REST AND HEAL

I BLEW A KISS INTO THE AIR
AND CALLED THE WIND
TO SEND IT THERE

SO IF A KISS
FALLS FROM THE SKY
YOU FEEL ME THERE
BUT DON'T
KNOW WHY

IT'S JUST A KISS
FROM ME TO YOU

I TALK TO MYSELF
'CAUSE I KNOW
YOU CAN HEAR

MY SWEET
LITTLE NOTHINGS
THAT TICKLE
YOUR EAR

LIKE A
TINY BLUE BIRD
ON A BRIGHT
SUMMERS DAY

SINGING
MY LOVE
AND THEN
FLYING AWAY

YOU DON'T BELIEVE
IN SUCH THINGS
AS TRUE LOVE

DON'T THINK LOVE
IS SENT
FROM HEAVEN ABOVE

IT SEEMS LIKE
YOU'RE SCARED
YOU DON'T HAVE
MUCH TO SAY

THE CLOSER I GET
THE MORE YOU
RUN AWAY

THIS LOVE IS INTENSE
IT CAUSES YOU FEAR
YOU PUSH ME AWAY
WHEN I WANT TO
BE NEAR

YOU LOOK IN
THE MIRROR
MY EYES
LOOK AT YOU

YOU THINK
TO YOURSELF
SHE'S TOO GOOD
TO BE TRUE

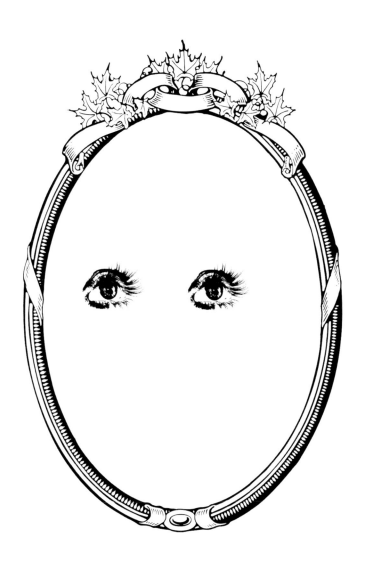

YOUR SILENCE IS BURNING
LEAVING SCARS ON MY HEART
IT STARTED BRIGHT RED
NOW IT'S COVERED IN DARK

SMOKING LIKE RIBS
ON A HOT BARBECUE
MY BARE NAKED SOUL
COVERED ONLY WITH YOU

THE SMOKE FILLS THE AIR
FOR MILES AROUND
BURNING FLESH
SECRET SAUCE
HAS THEM
CIRCLING AROUND

DO I MAKE YOUR
MOUTH WATER?
HOW LONG SHOULD
I BURN?

MY HEART'S
IN YOUR HAND
AS I WAIT
FOR MY TURN

YOU COVER ME UP
BUT I'M STILL
YOUR TATTOO

YOU CAN'T WASH
ME OFF
I'M FOREVER
WITH YOU

YOU SEE ME
IN THE MIRROR
WHEN YOU
TAKE OFF YOUR
CLOTHES

I COVER
YOUR LIPS
PAINT YOUR CHEST
AND
YOUR TOES

ON YOUR THIGHS
ON YOUR NECK
EVERY NOOK
EVERY CRACK

YOUR FAVORITE
MISTAKE
YOU CAN NEVER
TAKE BACK

A SECRET LOVE
NO ONE CAN KNOW
'CEPT I HAD YOU FIRST
SO LONG AGO

IN THE DARK
IN A CAR
THE HOTEL
WITH THE BAR

I HAD YOU FIRST
AND I KNOW
WHO YOU ARE

YOU ARE MINE
WHEN YOU'RE LYING
YES YOU LIE
TO YOURSELF

YOU ARE MINE
WHEN YOU'RE LYING
TO EVERYONE
ELSE

YOU'RE NOT HERS
YOU'RE NOT HIS
'CAUSE YOU'LL ALWAYS
BE MINE

NOT SOME GUY
IN A SUIT
YOU'RE A
BEAUTIFUL LION

YOU PURR
LIKE A CAT
YOU GROWL
AND YOU ROAR

YOU COME
AND YOU GO
THEN YOU COME
BACK FOR MORE

YOU GRAB ME
JUST RIGHT
AND YOU KNOW
WHERE TO BITE

MY
BEAUTIFUL LION
ONLY COMES OUT
AT NIGHT

I'LL BE OK
WITHOUT YOU
I'LL DO THE
BEST I CAN

BECAUSE I KNOW
A BETTER ME
MAKES YOU
A BETTER MAN

LIKE A
PREGNANT MOM
EATS HEALTHY
FOR HER
NEWBORN SON

I'M GROWING
FOR THE TWO OF US
THE TWO OF US
ARE ONE

MY SWEET TWIN FLAME
MY MIRROR
I'M READY
FOR YOUR RETURN

UNTIL THE DAY
I GET YOU BACK
MY LOVE FOR YOU
WILL BURN

LIKE BUTTERY
CARAMEL
ON A WARM
SUMMER DAY

THE LOOK
IN YOUR EYES
HAS ME
MELTING AWAY

STICKY
AND SWEET
AND EASY
TO CHEW

I'M
CARAMEL
YOU'RE
ICE CREAM

I'M MELTING
YOU TOO

I HEAR THE RAIN
AND EVERY DROP

IS LIKE A SWEET
FORGET ME NOT

EACH TAP UPON
MY WINDOW PANE

IS A LOVE NOTE
FROM YOU

THAT'S WRITTEN
IN RAIN

UP IN THE AIR
ARE YOU IN
OR YOU OUT?

I'M SO TIRED
OF WAITING

TO SEE WHAT
YOU'RE ABOUT

FEELING
SO LOST

THERE'S A
LESSON TO
LEARN

I DON'T KNOW
WHAT IT IS

WHEN WILL I
HAVE A TURN?

IF I DRIVE
SEVEN HOURS
I CAN GET TO
YOUR TOUCH

WHERE'S THE
MAGIC CARPET,
THAT I NEED
SO MUCH?

I COULD BE THERE
IN AN HOUR
AT MOST
MAYBE TWO

I FEEL LIKE
I'M CLOSE
BUT YET
SO FAR
FROM YOU

I WAKE UP AGAIN
IT'S A QUARTER
TO THREE

AM I WAKING YOU UP
OR, ARE YOU WAKING ME?

IT'S 2:45
BABE PLEASE
GO BACK TO SLEEP

AND STOP
MAKING PROMISES
YOU'RE NOT HERE
TO KEEP

YOUR LOVE IS LIKE
AN IMAGINARY
FRIEND

HERE TODAY
THEN GONE
AGAIN

CAN'T HEAR
YOUR VOICE
OR SEE
YOUR FACE

TEXTS ARE TAKING
REAL LOVES
PLACE

THINKING OF YOU
HAS GOT ME SO HIGH
I CAN'T COME BACK DOWN
AS HARD AS I TRY

THE THOUGHT
OF YOUR EYES
KEEPS ME UP
IN THE AIR

I STILL SMELL
YOUR SKIN
EVEN THOUGH
YOU'RE NOT HERE

I'M HIGH
ON YOUR LOVE
LIKE LEAVES
ON A TREE

TELL ME MY LOVE
ARE YOU THINKING
OF ME?

YOU SAY
YOU MISS ME
AND I MELT

THE GREATEST
LOVE
I'VE EVER FELT

THE SWEETEST LIPS
I'VE EVER KISSED

THE GREATEST LOVE
I'VE EVER MISSED

IF I COULD RUN
I'D RUN TO YOU
I'D CLIMB
THE HIGHEST
MOUNTAIN TOO

I'D RUN JUST LIKE
I DID BEFORE
BUT I CAN'T RUN
NOT ANYMORE

INSTEAD I'LL WALK
AND LIMP AND CRAWL
IF YOU'LL JUST
CATCH ME
WHEN I FALL

DON'T BE SAD
IT'LL BE OK
TOMORROW'S FINE
IF NOT TODAY

TIME WILL HEAL
ALL THAT WE'VE LOST
BUT FIRST WE HAVE
TO PAY THE COST

RIGHT OUR WRONGS
CLEAN THINGS
WE'VE MESSED

AND THROUGH
TRUE LOVE
WE WILL BE
BLESSED

WHEELS
ON THE GROUND

WHEN THE PLANE
TOUCHES DOWN

I HOPE THAT
YOU'RE READY

FOR SOME
FOOLING AROUND

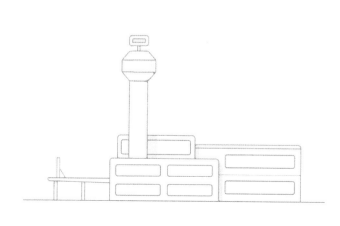

HIDING AWAY
IN MY BEDROOM
ALL DAY

IF I CAN'T
PLAY WITH YOU
THEN I DON'T
WANT TO PLAY

I WANT TO SWIM
DEEP IN YOUR SOUL
THE PLACE WHERE
NO ONE ELSE CAN GO

I WANT TO BE YOUR
DREAM COME TRUE
THE DREAM THAT'S
DEEP INSIDE OF YOU

SO DEEP INSIDE
YOU THOUGHT IT GONE
THE FASTEST RIDE
YOUR FAVORITE SONG

I WANT TO BE
YOUR DREAM COME TRUE
A SECRET WISH
MADE JUST FOR YOU

MAYBE WE SHOULD QUIT

WHILE WE'RE AHEAD

MAYBE WE SHOULD PUT

THIS LOVE TO BED

YOU GOT EVERYTHING YOU WANTED

I KNEW YOU WOULD

I SHOULD LET YOU GO

FOR YOUR OWN GOOD

I CAN GIVE YOU LOVE

LOVE'S NOT ENOUGH

YOU NEED TO GET GOING

BEFORE THE GOING

GETS TOUGH

I AM WHOLE
HAVE ALL I NEED

BUT WHEN YOU'RE GONE
MY HEART STILL BLEEDS

YOU TAKE A PIECE
WITH EACH GOODBYE

IT HURTS A BIT
IT MAKES ME CRY

I STITCH IT UP
AND LET IT MEND

WHEN YOU GET BACK
I'LL LOVE AGAIN

TUMERIC IN THE AIR
IVORY SOAP

A CASHMERE BLANKET
WRAPS US TOGETHER
LIKE A SHAWARMA

YOUR EYES
SO DEEP

FLOATING
EYES ON THE CEILING
I'M GONE

DIZZY

WEAK

GONE

I STARE AT YOUR EYES
FOR HOURS

ZOOM IN
ZOOM OUT

MY ONLINE LOVER
MY TOWER

I SEARCH
WHAT YOU'RE ABOUT

MY CASTLE IS
FALLING AROUND ME

I STARE AT MY PHONE
WHILE IT BURNS

THE ANGELS OF
LOVE ALL SURROUND ME

HOLD ME UP
'TIL MY TWINFLAME
RETURNS

YOUR PRETTY
BROWN FEET
THAT LITTLE
BLACK DOT

ON YOUR PRETTY
BROWN ANKLE
I MISS IT A LOT

I MISS RUBBING
YOUR FEET
AND KISSING
YOUR TOES

I NEED YOUR LOVE
LIKE A VASE
NEEDS A ROSE

MASTERED PATIENCE
MASTERED TIME
OPEN EYED
YOU'LL SOON BE MINE

SOON MEANS WHEN
THE TIME IS RIGHT
A THOUSAND YEARS
OR JUST ONE NIGHT

I'LL WAIT
AS I HAVE
ALWAYS DONE

I'LL WAIT BECAUSE
WE TWO
ARE ONE

I BELIEVE IN YOU
I BELIEVE IN ME
I BELIEVE IN THINGS
I CANNOT SEE

IN MIRACLES
IN HAPPY RAIN
IN HEARTS DESIRES
THAT GROW FROM
PAIN

IN MOUNTAINS MOVED
IN OCEANS SWAM
I BELIEVE 'CAUSE
THAT'S JUST WHO
I AM

BUT I KNOW
YOU DON'T

I UNDERSTAND

I DREAM ALONE
IN LALA LAND

YOU HIDE YOUR TEARS
BUT I CAN SEE
WHEN I SLEEP
YOU CALL TO ME

MY T-SHIRT'S WET
FROM TEARS YOU CRY
IN MY DREAMS
I WIPE YOUR EYES

HOPES AND TEARS
AND LOVE YOU SPEAK
YOU TELL ME SECRETS
THAT I KEEP

I'LL NEVER TELL
NOT EVEN YOU
THE THINGS
IN DREAMS
I SEE YOU DO

YOU'RE A MAN
BRAVE AND STRONG
HUSH MY LOVE
THERE'S NOTHING WRONG

LET'S GO FOR A RIDE
ROLL THE WINDOWS DOWN
TURN UP THE MUSIC
AND CIRCLE THE TOWN

HOLD MY HAND
AND SQUEEZE IT TIGHT
I'LL KISS YOUR NECK
WE'LL TALK ALL NIGHT

BE MY MAN
I'LL BE YOUR GIRL
LET'S GO FOR A RIDE
AROUND THE WORLD

LOVE ME LIKE
WHEN I WAS A CHILD
INNOCENT AND SWEET
FREE AND WILD

LET'S GET IN THE CAR
AND TURN THE KEY
ANYWHERE YOU WANT
JUST YOU AND ME

Made in the USA
Middletown, DE
07 July 2024